THE LAND OF TWYDELL AND THE DRAGON EGG

Tales of Avalon

Book 2 in the Tales of Avalon Series

Daisy Bourne

authorHOUSE®

AuthorHouse™ UK
1663 Liberty Drive
Bloomington, IN 47403 USA
www.authorhouse.co.uk
Phone: 0800.197.4150

Published by AuthorHouse 09/07/2016

ISBN: 978-1-5246-3651-7 (sc)
ISBN: 978-1-5246-3652-4 (hc)
ISBN: 978-1-5246-3653-1 (e)

Library of Congress Control Number: 2016914489

Print information available on the last page.

This book is printed on acid-free paper.

Illustrations by Schenker De Leon

CONTENTS

For our grandchildren,
Jake and Alfie,
with special thanks to Jake
for being the first child
to read the draft of this book

CHARACTERS

List of main characters, in alphabetical order:

Ajax: green dragon; husband of Blitzen

Alexander: the blacksmith's son (usually referred to as Alex); brother of Andrew; friend of Edward.

Alfred: an elf

Allarond: King of the Elves

Andrew: the blacksmith's son; brother of Alexander; friend of Edward.

Arthur: King of Avalon (formerly, King of Briton); husband of Gilda the witch; father of Edward and Rosalie.

Azgoose: a witch who can create clouds of goo

Bizzbuzz: a wizard who specialises in making honey

Blitzen: blue Dragon; wife of Ajax

Bramble Family: Bertha (Great-Grandmother Bramble), mother of Nora (Grandmother Bramble) and Maura; Nora (Grandmother Bramble), mother of Dilly, Dally, and Sally; Dilly Bramble, wife of Jerry; Dally Bramble, wife of Garod; Sally Bramble, wife of Isaiah and mother of Heather

Bertha (Great-Grandmother Bramble) m. Barley

|

Maura and Nora (Grandmother Bramble) m. Dillbert

|

Dilly m. Jerry Dally m. Garod Sally m. Isaiah

|

Heather

Comet: Merlin's white stallion

Connie: the baker's daughter

Daisy: the last of the Brewins

Derrick: Prince of Twydell; son of King Frederrick and Queen Elise

Edward-Arthur: illegitimate son of King Arthur (usually referred to simply as Edward)

Elise: wife/consort of King Frederrick of Twydell (given the title of queen at the time of marriage)

Elvira: Queen of the Witches; all her witches migrated to Avalon

Esmerelda: Queen of the Witches (after Elvira); daughter of Elvira

Farainne: wife/consort of Allarond, King of the Elves (given the title of queen at the time of marriage)

Frederrick: King of Twydell

Gilda: one of the first witches to migrate to Avalon; she later married King Arthur; mother of Rosalie

Greatog: former leader of the giants; killed in an earlier battle with the Trajaens; father of Zog

Helen-Joy: a soothsayer

Jeanette: Princess of Twydell; daughter of King Frederrick and Queen Elise

Jeffrey: King of Kerner

Jonathan: a young warlock who specialises in plants (herbologist); son of the wizard Yzor and a half-witch

Lennox: last of the unicorns of Earth

Maud: Queen of the Fairies; married to Selogon

Merlin: powerful wizard who organised the migration to Avalon; advisor to King Arthur

Rabbart lll: King of Barrmin

Rosalie: daughter of King Arthur and Gilda the witch

Selogon: husband/consort of Maud, Queen of the Fairies

Shirley-Poppy: wife/consort of Jeffrey, King of Kerner (given the title of queen at the time of marriage)

Steven: Prince of Kerner; son of King Jeffrey and Queen Shirley-Poppy

Tannitus: powerful wizard; father of Tannus

Tannus: powerful young warlock; son of Tannitus

Willy the Wood Wizard: wizard who can talk to trees

Wormald the Wise: wise old wizard

Yzor: a wizard who specialises in plants (herbologist); father of Jonathan

Zog: leader of the giants; son of Greatog

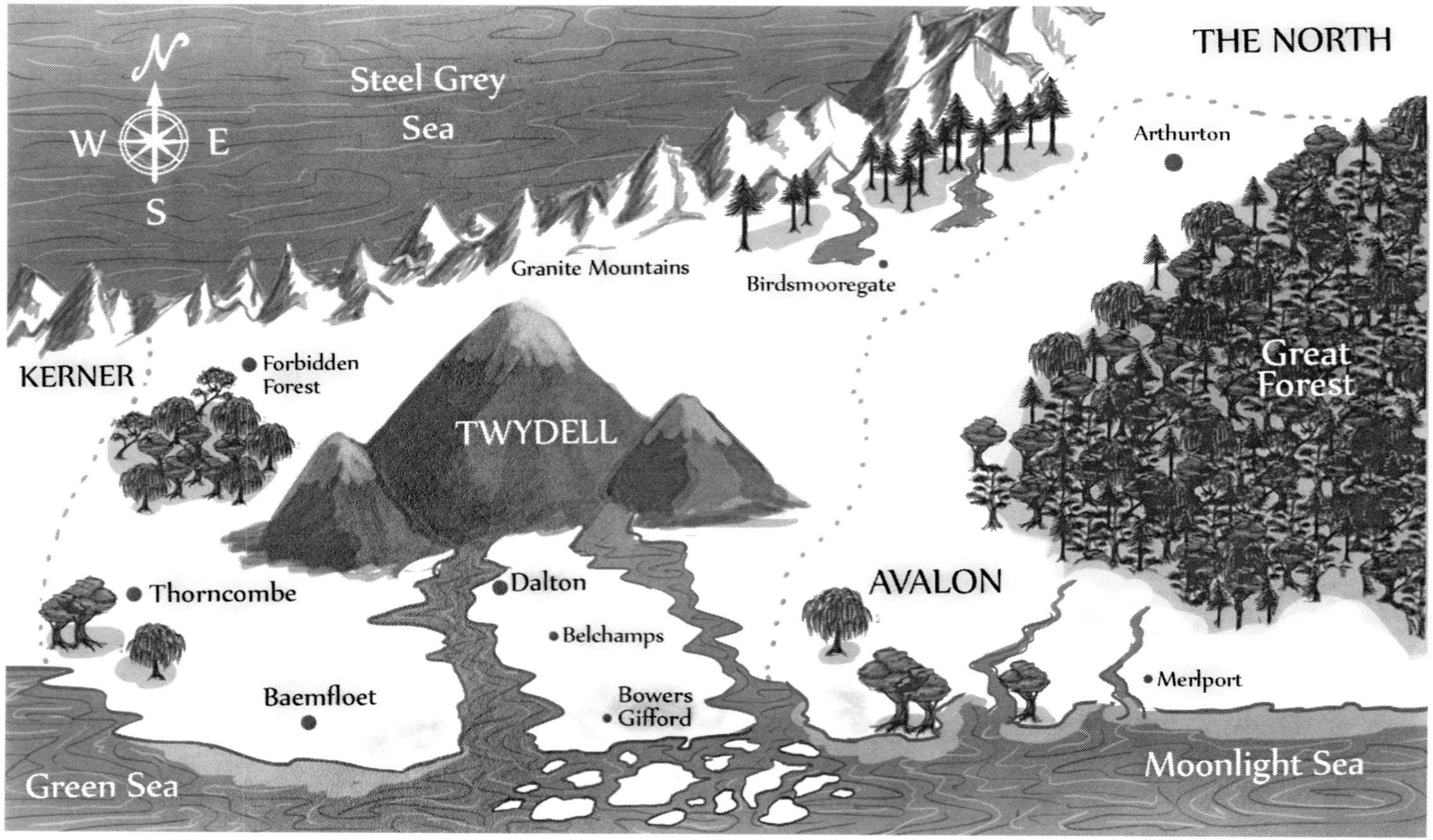
N
W
E
S
Steel Grey
Sea
THE NORTH
Granite Mountains
Birdsmooregate
Arthurton
KERNER
Forbidden
Forest
TWYDELL
Great
Forest
Thorncombe
Dalton
AVALON
Belchamps
Baemfloet
Bowers
Gifford
Merlport
Green Sea
Moonlight Sea

PROLOGUE

For those who have not read *The New Land,* book 1 in the *Tales of Avalon* series, this is a brief outline of the story so far. It is much better to read the first book before this one, though; otherwise, you will miss much excitement and adventure!

Many witches, wizards, fairies, and humans had left their home in Briton to live in a new land found by Merlin. The name of the land was Avalon. It was hoped that Avalon would be a happy and peaceful place, without the fear of persecution which so many magical beings had endured on earth.

Avalon itself was a happy place. The newcomers made friends with the giants who lived in the Great Forest. The giants came to the aid of the Avalonians when they were attacked by the marauding Trajaens, a race of people who appeared to live on the sea.

This second book in the *Tales of Avalon* series, *The Land of Twydell and the Dragon Egg,* finds the Avalonians, who live in the small settlement known as Merlport, recovering from the battle with the Trajaens.

Merlin was away on a visit to neighbouring Twydell when this battle started, but he returned just as the battle was ending. The mighty wizard and the six Twydell soldiers escorting him then entered the battle, helping to bring it to a speedy and successful conclusion.

The day after the battle, the leaders of the inhabitants of Avalon met to discuss what to do next. They were also keen to hear what adventures had befallen Merlin in neighbouring Twydell, and why he had been gone longer than expected. It is during this meeting that this book begins.

CHAPTER 1

The Demise of Twydell

The leaders discussed the terrible happenings of the previous day. Tears were shed for those who had been lost. A plan of action was put together to help protect Merlport if the Trajaens broke their promise not to return. The leaders had taken a break from the meeting to partake in refreshment, but they were now seated again, anxious to hear about Merlin's adventures in neighbouring Twydell.

King Arthur; Esmerelda, now Queen of the Witches; Maud, Queen of the Fairies; and Allarond, King of the Elves all sat at Arthur's round table.

Prince Edward was also invited to the meeting. Edward's invitation was significant. Arthur had suffered many battle injuries during his lifetime. Yesterday's fight with the Trajaens had been no different: he had suffered a deep sword slash to his leg. The ageing king was pale, and all noticed how he winced with pain at even the slightest movement. Edward's presence identified him as the next leader of the humans in Avalon.

Merlin took a long swig of apple juice before beginning his tale.

The wizard started by describing that he had borrowed Willy the Wood Wizard's broom and flown in the direction of the country which neighboured Avalon. He then gave a brief overview of the land known as Twydell. The country's name meant "two valleys" in an ancient language – *twy* meaning "two", and *dell* meaning "valley". Merlin had flown further inland than he had ever ventured since coming to Avalon. He had also flown very high, and in the distance, could see three sprawling mountains with two valleys between them. It was obvious as to how the land had got its name. However, the kingdom was much larger than just the mountains and the two valleys. There were meadows which swept down to the sea. But the land near the sea bordering Avalon was very marshy, and small islands dotted the water round the coast. To the west of Twydell, near the border with the land of Kerner, stood a small forest.

The capital of Twydell was called Dalton, but there were also several towns and large villages in the country. Baemfloet was a small town which stood on the coast, guarding the country against the Trajaens. Bowers Gifford was a large village which stood near the marshes. Thorncombe was another small town; it had a busy farming community near the small forest, and traded much of its produce with Kerner. Birdsmoorgate, another farming community near the border with the north, used to do a lot of trade with the northerners but now did very little business with them. The northerners had worked hard to develop arable land and now grew sufficient crops for themselves, so Birdsmoorgate was left with little trade.

Merlin had learnt there was a lot of infighting between the people of the north in years gone by. The north had once been made up of several different kingdoms. Now they had all come under one leader. The ancestors of some of the northern kingdoms had been friendly with the Twydellers, but the new regime did not like people from the south crossing its borders. There had also been some trouble between the northerners and the Brewins, but the people of Twydell didn't know much about what had happened.

The Twydellers had little to do with the Brewins, who liked to keep to themselves. The Twydellers regarded this to be a pity. If the two countries had joined forces, they might have been able to defend themselves better against the Trajaens.

Having described the land neighbouring Avalon to his fellow leaders, Merlin took another swig of apple juice before telling them about the rest of his eventful journey to Twydell.

"It's been a long time since I travelled by broom. It makes my old bones ache, sitting for hours on that thin handle and bending forward to hold on to its end. I must admit, though, I had forgotten how good it is to see the sunrise from above and feel a light breeze blowing in my face.

"I was enjoying my bird's-eye view, watching the herds of animals make their way along the plains, when I spotted a long trail of people. I steered the broom a little closer, and could see that some were carrying bags or trundling wheelbarrows with what appeared to be their possessions inside. Some rode on horses, and others rode in carts drawn by oxen or ponies, but most were on foot.

"I flew down to speak to the people, but they were startled to see me. I suppose the sight of a man riding a broomstick must be a curious sight to any human other than an Avalonian. I tried to call out a greeting, but they picked up stones and threw them at me. I knew the stones couldn't reach me, but when I saw one preparing to fire an arrow at me, well, that was another matter. I flew up high, out of reach, and travelled on towards Dalton.

"I needed to talk to someone to find out what was going on. Eventually, I spotted a small family travelling together. The man was pushing a cart, and there were two small children with the woman. I guessed that the children had not been able to keep pace with the other travellers, so they had fallen behind. They didn't appear to be armed, so I swooped down, landing on the road in front of them."

Merlin smiled as he related their reactions to him dropping out of the sky and onto the road: the man's jaw dropped, and the woman screamed; however, the children only laughed.

"Good day, young sir and young lady." The wizard bowed his head in greeting to the young family. "I am on my way to Dalton, the capital of Twydell, and want to make sure that I am travelling in the right direction."

The man and woman continued to stare in disbelief.

"Would you like to share my lunch with me?" Merlin opened the bundle he was carrying on his back, to reveal a loaf of bread, a wedge of cheese, and a red apple.

It was obvious that the children had been crying. Tears had left clean trails down their dirty, travel-stained faces. They looked eagerly at the food the strange old man offered, and ran to take it.

"Don't touch it!" shouted the mother as she moved between her children and the wizard. "It might be poisoned."

The children looked bewildered. The food looked so tempting, but their mother was usually right.

Merlin smiled. "My food has not been poisoned." He took the cloth in which the food had been bundled, spreading the fabric on the ground and laying the food on top. He drew a small knife from his pocket, pulled a bite-sized piece of bread from the loaf, and cut a small piece of cheese from the wedge. He squeezed the cheese between the bread and popped it into his mouth.

"What do you want from us?" asked the man nervously as his eyes looked longingly at the food.

"I only want to know why so many people appear to be travelling away from Dalton, taking all their belongings with them." Merlin cast his eye over the contents of the cart. There were some cooking pots; what appeared to be dirty folded blankets; and a heap of clothes which appeared to be damp because they left water stains on the edge of the cart.

"We are leaving Dalton because it has become a dangerous place to live. We have lost everything we owned. Now we are travelling to Birdsmoorgate, as far away from Dalton as we can get without entering the north. We pray that we will find safety there."

Merlin noticed that the young man's hair was matted with what appeared to be mud. All the family wore mud-splattered clothing. "Please tell me what has happened in Dalton. You can rest awhile and share my lunch. You can then resume your journey feeling a little refreshed."

Although the father and mother were still wary of the oddly clad man who had flown down from the sky on a broomstick, they accepted his offer. They were amazed when Merlin pulled a short stick from his pocket and, waving it over the food, doubled the size of the bread and wedge of cheese. Another apple appeared from nowhere. Another wave of his wand, and the quantity doubled again.

"There! That should be enough to go round. Please help yourselves."

"How did you do that?" asked the woman, her mouth gaping.

"I am a wizard," explained Merlin. "I can do all sorts of magic tricks. Doubling food is one of them."

As they tucked into lunch, Merlin told the young family about Avalon and his mission to speak to King Frederrick.

He asked them again about why so many people appeared to be travelling east, with all their possessions in tow. "What is it that has frightened you so much that you feel the need to leave your homes?" he asked.

The young couple looked downhearted. Tears started to run freely down their despondent faces. They said that a pair of dragons lived in the central mountain just above Dalton. Dragons had lived there for as long as anyone could remember, and they had never bothered the Daltonians.

"Now and then, when we went fishing, we used to see them skimming across the mountain lakes, taking fish for themselves," the young father remembered sadly. "We would hide in one of the caves or in the trees, and watch. Afterwards, we would rush to swim in the lake because the flames from the dragons' breath heated the water. They never harmed us, and we used to look forward to seeing them. Sometimes we thought they warmed the water just to amuse us."

The young father went on to tell Merlin that suddenly, and for no apparent reason, the dragons started attacking the Twydell towns and villages. Tears filled the man's eyes as he remembered the terrible night not that long ago, when the thatch on his family's cottage roof caught fire, and he and his wife and children had to run for their lives. Many other families suffered the same fate. The townsfolk worked together to put out the fires, forming a human chain to carry buckets of water back and forth from the river.

No sooner had they put the fires out than a thunderbird appeared in the sky, bringing with it a strong wind and an assembly of dark clouds. Very few people had ever seen such a huge bird before, and no one knew where it had come from. As the dark clouds blew across Dalton, a heavy storm erupted. Thunder clapped, and lightning zigzagged its sharp, bright needles above the town. A lamb ran from a burning barn, and the thunderbird picked the creature up in its talons, carrying it off and flying back in the direction from which it had come.

Although the thunderbird disappeared into the distance, the storm continued. The palace was struck by a fierce streak of lightning, which brought down part of the wall surrounding the courtyard. The river filled with rain and burst its banks. Many of the young family's possessions which had not been devastated by fire were destroyed by the flood.

The king organised some temporary shelter for the homeless families, but even that was destroyed.

The two-pronged attack – the dragon's fire, followed by the thunderbird's storm – happened time and again. Reluctantly, people began leaving their homes to find new settlements where there were no dragons or thunderbirds.

Merlin thanked the young couple for the information. He conjured up some more food for the family before parting. He would like to have provided more but explained that performing magic spells was tiring and he needed to preserve his energy for the rest of his trip. He suggested that the young couple might find safety in Avalon.

Wishing the young family well and bidding them goodbye, Merlin continued on his journey to Dalton.

As he neared the capital of Twydell, Merlin was shocked to see the devastation below. Some houses quenched of flames still smouldered. Smoke billowed in grey ribbons into the sky, forming a smoky haze that smelt most unpleasant. The remains of other houses, which had been burnt to the ground, were now covered in thick mud. Old people, too frail to travel, were sitting or standing in what was left of the palace courtyard. They sat there, hoping that the king would provide them with food and shelter. Soldiers were trying to set up makeshift tents. The palace itself, and other more ornate marquees, appeared to have been put to use as a hospital for the sick and injured.

Merlin walked to the palace door, but armed guards stopped him. He asked to speak to the king, but the guards just laughed. The old wizard was dressed in his travelling attire of a long grey woollen cloak and a tall grey hat; his waist-length grey hair and long grey beard were tangled from his long days of travelling on the broom. He carried the broom in one hand and his wooden staff in the other. The soldiers made fun of the new arrival's bedraggled appearance, telling him that the king would have no time for such a strange-looking person.

The sorcerer ignored the guards' mockery. "Tell the king that I am Merlin, a wizard well respected by Arthur, king of your neighbouring land. This was once known as Brewin but is now named Avalon. Tell King Frederrick that I can talk to dragons and will try to speak to the angry beast before it attacks again."

The soldiers did not believe the unkempt traveller in front of them. They thought he was some kind of fool. They laughed loudly as they pushed him down the steps of the outer hall, back into the courtyard.

"If you can really speak to dragons," one of the soldiers yelled, "you'd better go and find them, and tell them to keep away from Dalton! If you come back here, we'll throw you into one of our dungeons."

Merlin walked back into the town and did his best to mingle with the people milling about in the streets. At the outset, people were cautious and reluctant to speak to the peculiar stranger, but when he showed how his magic could help them, they started to befriend him. He cast a spell which created a light wind that dried clothing soaked by the rain. He found a child who had been parted from his parents. One of his spells helped lift a cart which had turned on its side and got stuck in the mud.

The stories told by the townsfolk were the same as that told by the young family he had met. No one knew why the dragons had started to attack the Twydellers. Nobody knew where the thunderbird had come from, as its like had not been seen for many years.

Merlin learnt that people of magic had been shunned and driven from the town many years ago. The Twydellers believed that there were still some people of magic living in the Forbidden Forest, which lay on the border with Kerner. The forest was forbidden because those who tried to enter were trapped in a binding plant which wrapped itself round their bodies. Several townsfolk knew people who had tried to enter the forest and escaped only by hacking themselves free of the weed. They had heard stories that the creeping bindweed could grow two or three feet in a matter of minutes. There were stories that people determined to enter the forest had been suffocated in the coils of the deadly binding weed. The forest had indeed forbidden anyone to enter its depths.

Merlin was resting with other folk on the town's walls when he heard the warning blast of a guardsman's horn. Terrified people ran for cover, and children screamed. Merlin turned to see a large green dragon in the distance, heading towards Dalton. He placed his staff in the long hidden pocket inside his travelling gown, and then mounted Willy's broomstick. The old wizard soared high in the air, flying his borrowed broom in the direction of the oncoming dragon.

People hesitated from pursuing their search for shelter. They pointed at the strange man flying through the air, on a broomstick, towards their deadly enemy. The guards who had ridiculed Merlin stood at their posts, with jaws dropped and mouths wide open.

As Merlin drew close to the dragon, he raised his arms to show that he carried no weapons. However, the gesture seemed meaningless to the dragon, which blew forth a trail of fiery red flames. Merlin lowered his arms and expertly steered the broom above the dragon, missing the deadly flames aimed at him. The dragon turned, ready to blow forth its deadly flames again, but before it could exhale its fire, Merlin shouted to it in a language it would understand.

"I am no enemy of the dragon. I seek only to speak to you."

The dragon hesitated for a moment, hovering in the air. "Well, I have never seen a man flying through the air on a brush before. Nor have I ever heard a man who spoke our language. Therefore, I will allow you to speak. But, I warn you, I am angry, and in a hurry to hurt those who have hurt us. I have no time for idle chit-chat!"

"I am Merlin. I came from an unhappy land far away to live in a world where mankind could live in peace and harmony with nature. I am told that the dragons have lived near the people of Twydell for many years, and neither has bothered the other. Please tell me, my friend, what has happened to make you so angry that you wish to harm the people of Dalton? What have they done to you?"

"They stole our egg. My wife and I have waited years for a child. She laid an egg and guarded it well. But then, one day, while I was out looking for food, she left the nest. She was not away for long, but when she got back, our precious egg was gone. The people stole it, and now they must either give it back, unharmed, or suffer the consequences."

"But, my dear dragon, the people to whom I have spoken know nothing of your egg. Why do you think that it is they who stole it?"

"Who else could have stolen it? A cow could not carry any egg, nor could a goat or a horse or a sheep!"

Merlin nodded. "If someone stole your egg, then whoever it is does indeed deserve to be punished. However, surely not every single person who lives in Twydell."

"All who stay will be punished, including you!" The dragon took a deep breath, ready to breathe out fire again.

Merlin rose swiftly into the air. "Allow me to speak a little longer!" he cried. "I may be able to help you."

The dragon continued to hover. "Speak."

"Let me go back to Dalton. I will speak to King Frederrick, asking him to search every home, shed, and barn in his country to try to find your precious egg. If the egg is hidden in Twydell, and you keep burning the houses and barns, surely your egg will be destroyed too."

The dragon looked thoughtful for a moment, continuing to hover.

Merlin persisted. "Let me try to find your egg. I cannot promise that I will find it, but I swear that I will do my best. I need time, though, and so will King Frederrick. Sending his soldiers to search every nook and cranny will take weeks."

"You speak sense, strange man called Merlin," replied the dragon. "I cannot wait weeks, though. The next full moon is fifteen days hence; if our egg is not returned to me and my wife by then, we will destroy the town known as Dalton, and every other town in Twydell and Kerner."

"Thank you for listening to me." Merlin bowed his head in gratitude. "However, I beg you to consider that the egg may not have been taken by the Twydellers or the Kernans. I would like to speak to your wife so that I can try to put together the pieces of this puzzle for myself."

"Very well," replied the dragon. "She is in poor spirits, and the sight of a man flying on a brush, without wings, and who can speak our language, may amuse her. On the other hand, she is so angry that she may cook you alive in her fury."

"I will take that risk. I shall go now to King Frederrick and tell him of the truce we have agreed upon. I will then look forward to visiting you and your charming wife."

The two parted company. The dragon turned and flew back in the direction from whence it had come. Merlin steered his broomstick back to Dalton Palace as quickly as it could carry him. When he arrived, he did not need to look for the king, because the king was waiting for him in the courtyard, coming forward to meet him when he landed.

Frederrick was an old man whose face was pale and lined with worry. He wore no crown. He had spent much time in the town, comforting his people and organising shelter. His fine velvet gown was spattered with mud.

"So you are the man who said he could talk to dragons, but my guards did not believe you," said the king. "I would never have believed such a thing myself if I had not seen it with my very own eyes."

"Sire," said Merlin. He nodded his head to the king but did not bow. "The dragon believes that one the people of Twydell or Kerner has stolen his egg. The dragon has waited many years for his wife to bear the egg. The egg is precious to them, for dragon eggs are rare, and she will probably never lay another. He is furious. He has given us till the new moon to find his egg. If it is not found, I fear that your towns and the people who remain within them are doomed. I have told him that you would search every house and building in your land to find the egg."

"I will order every inch of Twydell to be searched," said the king. "Furthermore, I will offer a reward to anyone who can give us information as to where the egg might be. My people and I will do all we possibly can to find it."

"You must also send a message to King Jeffrey of Kerner, telling him to do the same."

"I shall do so straight away. Now tell me, strange man, will you help us search for the missing egg? Will you speak to the dragon again on our behalf?"

"My name is Merlin," the wizard said, correcting the king.

The king's pale cheeks reddened, but he smiled warmly.

"Ah, yes. My guards told me that you and a new king, Arthur, had settled in the land to the east of us. I look forward to meeting our new neighbours."

"King Arthur will look forward to meeting you, if you survive the revenge of the dragons. But now I would be grateful for some food and drink, and then I must go to meet the mother of the egg. I hope that she will agree to speak to me. It may not be one of your people, or indeed anyone from Kerner, who stole the egg, and I need to understand what happened."

King Frederrick invited Merlin into the castle. This time, the guards bowed respectfully as Merlin swept past them. Queen Elise ordered food and wine to be brought to the table in the king's parlour. The royal couple shared a hasty meal with Merlin before his departure, which gave them a little time to parley.

"Tell me, sire," said Merlin. "Is there a soothsayer in Dalton from whom I might seek advice?"

"A soothsayer! We do not encourage such nonsense here." The king stopped. "I apologise. Your kind has not been welcome here, but you have proved that you are a good man. I realise that you are trying to do all you can to help us, and did not mean to offend you. There has been no soothsayer here for many years. I believe there was a woman once, but my grandfather banished her. It is said that she went to live in the Forbidden Forest. She will be dead and gone by now, but she had a husband. It is possible, I suppose, that they had children who still live there, but I doubt it."

"Yes, the Forbidden Forest. Who will search that?" Merlin wanted to know.

"That cannot be searched," replied the king, "for no one who enters ever returns."

"Then that will be my task!" responded Merlin. "If I have my bearings right, I will need to travel north-west to the mountain to visit the home of the dragons, and from there, I will travel west to the Forbidden Forest."

"Your directions are correct, but I fear that I shall see you no more," the king said with regret. "For those who try to enter the Forbidden Forest suffocate in the creeping weeds that surround it."

"I hope that is not the case, and I hope that I will return to Dalton with good news. Now I must make haste. We both have much to do and little time in which to do it."

Thus, Merlin left Dalton. The king and his people wished him good luck as they waved goodbye. However, few believed that they would ever see the brave old wizard again.

CHAPTER 2

Ajax and Blitzen's Grief

Merlin flew to the mountain where the dragons lived. It did not take him long to find their cave. He simply looked for the red glow of fire.

First, he flew round the cave, to see how easy it would be to climb up to the entrance. The mountain was steep, and there was no pathway. It would have been very difficult for any man to climb up to the dragons' home, let alone leave carrying an egg.

Merlin flew to the entrance of the cave, feeling the heat exuding from within. He drew his staff and issued a cooling spell before calling out to say that he had arrived.

The deep voice of the male dragon bade him enter.

A fire shielded the cave from the cold outside. On the other side of the fire, the cave opened out into a large room.

In the middle of the room was a round nest made of straw and leaves. The dragons sat opposite each other on either side of the nest, looking sadly at the centre, where the straw had become depressed into an oval shape. Merlin guessed that this was where their precious egg had rested.

Whereas the male dragon was green, with lizard-like yellow eyes, the female dragon was dark blue, with eyes just a shade lighter. The blue dragon was some five feet shorter than her husband, who was thirty feet long. She was not as muscular as her husband, either; even so, she was a powerful force to be reckoned with.

"So you think you can find my egg?" she asked, without any hope in her voice. "We have unleashed our fury on the people of Twydell and Kerner, but it has not helped. We do not know what else to do. We never harmed any human beings. We used to like watching them swim in the lake after we had heated it for them with our fiery breath. Why would they want to hurt us so?"

"They believe that by stealing our egg, they will kill us off, as we will then have no children to replace us when we die!" the male dragon said angrily. As he spoke, he raised his tail and cracked it back down hard against the rock floor.

"I understand your anger," said Merlin. "But I have looked round, and can see no way that a man can easily climb up here. There is no path and, presumably, no other entrance."

"You got here," replied the female sharply as she fixed her cold blue eyes on the wizard.

"Yes, that is true," conceded Merlin. "But as I understand, it King Frederrick's ancestors banned people of magic from Twydell many years ago. Your husband has told me that he has seen no other people flying on broomsticks."

The blue dragon nodded slowly.

Merlin continued. "The king has ordered every building in his kingdom to be investigated, and he sent a message to King Jeffrey of Kerner, urging him to do the same. I will do my best to search the Forbidden Forest, where other men will not tread. Please, now, tell me what happened. I need to understand it all before I make my way to the forest."

Merlin learnt that the green male dragon was called Ajax, and his wife, the blue dragon, was called Blitzen. Dragons rarely lay eggs more than once in a lifetime, and the couple was delighted when Blitzen yielded her heart's desire. She made a comfy nest and rested the precious egg inside it. The egg would take nine months to hatch.

She sat on the egg, keeping it safe and warm, rarely leaving the nest for nearly seven months. Ajax brought her food – a task he found increasingly difficult, as Blitzen's tastes had changed since her pregnancy, even though she had laid the egg.

One day, she asked him for oysters, which could only be found on an island a longer distance away than he usually travelled. He was gone a long time, and Blitzen was hungry. She fancied some fresh air, and at the same time thought she would catch some fish in the lake. She thought it might be fun to watch the people swim after she had heated the water for them. However, by the time she got to the lake, storm clouds had started to form, and the fishermen had already left the lake to return to their homes. She caught a few fish as she skimmed across the water, and she decided to return home. However, she heard a clap of thunder, followed swiftly by a lightning streak, and decided to shelter in a nearby grotto until the storm had passed.

Blitzen told Merlin that by the time she got home, the egg was gone. She described how she flew frantically over the mountain, time and again, to see if the thief was still in view. However, she could see no one.

"So there were no people near the lake," said Merlin. "And you could see no one running from the mountain when you returned home."

"No one," Blitzen concurred.

"You say that there was a clap of thunder and then a streak of lightning?" Merlin's tone was gentle as he continued his questions. "Did you see any strange bird in the sky?"

"No." Tears dropped from Blitzen's huge, sad eyes as she shook her head. "I took cover until the rain stopped. It rained in torrents. I doubt whether even a clever man like you could fly in such a storm. Why, oh why, did I leave my nest?"

"I could not have flown in such a storm." The wizard tried to alleviate the poor creature's guilt. "I can only think of one creature which apparently can, although I have never seen one myself."

"The thunderbird!" Ajax jumped to his feet, and his tail rose again, quickly thumping back down on the floor, with a loud smack.

Merlin wondered why this repeated action left the dragon in no pain.

"I have seen the thunderbird flying towards the towns and villages after I have reaped my vengeance on them," Ajax said. "The bird brings with it thunder, lightning, and heavy rain!"

"It is possible the thunderbird is the culprit," said Merlin. "It could easily spot your cave from above because it exudes such a warm glow. We must not jump to conclusions, though. I must find this bird and speak to it. I hope I speak a language it understands."

"I have a language it understands," snarled Ajax as a long, sleek tongue of flame emitted from his mouth.

Even though the flame was not aimed at Merlin, the heat made the old wizard tremble, and he stepped backwards to avoid being burnt.

"I know you wish to question the thunderbird, but I am afraid that you will frighten it so much that it may lie to try to save itself," Merlin said. "Please let me speak to it. If, and I mean *if*, it is guilty, then perhaps I can persuade it to tell the truth."

Ajax and Merlin argued for some time. However, neither knew where the thunderbird lived, and without such knowledge, neither would be able to question it anyway.

Eventually, Merlin said, "I will travel to the Forbidden Forest and see if I can find anything there."

"How will you do that?" asked Blitzen. "Not even we can get near that forest. We have tried to land there, but the weeds entwine our wings and feet."

"Then best leave the Forbidden Forest to me, my dear," said Merlin. "You and Ajax can scan the mountains by flying high in the air. The thunderbird may just as easily nest in the mountains as in the forest. Now I will bid you goodnight. If I find anything in that mysterious piece of woodland, I will return immediately."

The dragons offered to let Merlin stay in their cave overnight, but he was anxious to get to the forest, which was a good night's journey away. He flew under the starry night, the gentle wind ruffling his hair and beard, his cape blowing behind him. He nearly fell asleep more than once, but woke with a start each time he felt himself slipping from the broom.

CHAPTER 3

The Forbidden Forest

As the sun rose up from behind the mountain, Merlin could see the Forbidden Forest in the distance. Trees nestled against the tall mountains which separated Twydell from Kerner. He brought the broomstick down at the edge of the forest and spent a few moments listening to the dawn chorus. He then drew his staff, which was concealed in the long pocket inside his cloak.

Sure enough, bindweed, as thick as rope, wound an intricate pattern round the forest. Merlin was considering what spell to use to cut away the powerful bindweed, when, suddenly, a patch of the plant unwound its vines to provide an opening.

The wizard hesitated, wondering if it was some kind of trap, and then he heard the sound of hooves approaching. He looked into the depth of the forest and saw a pale horse-like shape drawing close. As the shape drew nearer, he could see that it was not a horse, but his old friend Lennox, the pure white unicorn, who had travelled on one of the ships from Earth.

Merlin threw open his arms and wrapped them round the unicorn's neck. Lennox nuzzled up against the old wizard's face. Both felt the warmth of their genuine friendship.

"Well, my old friend, how glad I am to see you!" Merlin spoke in Unicornian, a language both he and Lennox understood.

"I am happy to see you too, my wise wizard. I am not a beast of burden, but, on this occasion, if you climb on my back, I will take you to the lady you seek."

Lennox lowered his front legs to make it easier for Merlin to climb on his back, but the old wizard hesitated.

"What lady?" Merlin asked.

"The lady who is expecting you. Climb on to my back. I have never offered to carry a human being before. If you do not wish to take up my offer, I will walk ahead, and you can follow."

Merlin climbed onto Lennox's back, thanking his friend for the lift. He was tired because he had travelled all night, and was most grateful to have the opportunity to ride. It was indeed a great privilege to be borne on the back of a unicorn, and much more comfortable than a broomstick handle.

As Lennox trotted into the forest, Merlin heard a rustle, and looked behind to see the entrance into the forest closing over. Lennox wound his way along a slim path with dense forest on either side. The bindweed formed a lace-like canopy over the top of the trees. In effect, the forest was sealed.

Lennox continued along the winding path for several hours, carrying Merlin on his back. It was early afternoon when they eventually reached a waterfall. An opening in the forest canopy, just in front of the waterfall, allowed an expanse of grass to grow. A small herd of unicorns grazed in this small pasture.

"These are my wives," said Lennox.

Merlin raised his eyebrows. "Congratulations! A fine herd you have here. I don't believe I have ever seen such an excellent brood of mares!"

A chestnut mare with a silver mane and a white blaze on her face whinnied, as if to acknowledge Merlin's comments.

"And this is where you dismount, my wise wizard. The lady you seek awaits you. She lives in the cave behind the waterfall."

The old wizard slid down from the unicorn's back and, after thanking the unicorn, carefully made his way up the steps in the rocks, which led to a hollow behind the waterfall.

"Merlin! At last we meet! I've been waiting to meet you for a long time." A slim, handsome woman, wearing a cream smock over a floral blouse, stepped out of the entrance behind the waterfall.

The wizard squinted because a rainbow had appeared in the waterfall between him and the person greeting him. Through the rainbow he could see that she wore a colourful scarf round her hair and gold hooped earrings which glinted in the sun. The arm she extended was covered in gold bracelets, which jangled as she extended her hand. She reminded him of a Gypsy.

"Greetings, my lady." Merlin bowed respectfully as he took her hand. "I am sorry. I do not know your name, nor did I realise that anyone was expecting me."

"Come in, come in. You must be tired. You've been travelling all night and not had much rest for many days. I've been watching you. Here, have a cup of hot mint tea – I find it so refreshing. I have a plate of fresh fruit and vegetables prepared for you too."

Before Merlin could ask who she was, or how she knew he was coming, he was ushered into the cave and told to sit on a patchwork quilt. The mysterious woman served him a cup of hot brew, and provided bowls of delicious fruits and vegetables. Despite being widely travelled, Merlin had never seen the like of some of the fruits he was offered. The bowls contained ripe peaches, grapes of both black and green varieties, oranges, cherries, and plums, plus raw carrots and cucumber.

"This is delicious!" said Merlin, who was very hungry. The first genuine smile in a long time cracked his wrinkled old face, and his blue eyes twinkled. "Where did you get this wonderful fruit? I've never tasted anything like it before."

"I'll show you later," replied the Gypsy-looking woman as she munched on a carrot.

"Ah, I see now. You are a soothsayer." Merlin noticed a table on which stood a round object covered by a purple velvet cloth. Spread next to the object were cards illustrated with colourful pictures. Merlin recognised the shape of a crystal ball and the images of the Tarot cards.

"Very observant of you! I am Helen-Joy."

"What a lovely name," said Merlin, who had taken an instant liking to the woman sitting in front of him, sharing the plate of fruit and vegetables.

"My parents couldn't decide whether to name me Helen, after a mythical queen, or Joy, because I was always happy. They ended up giving me a double name."

"How long have you lived here?"

"I was banished from Dalton by King Frederrick's grandfather almost eighty years ago. I came here with my dearest husband, Bryan, who was a minstrel. He could have stayed in Dalton, you know, but he chose to leave his friends and family and to follow me here. We were so happy, but Bryan is gone. He died more than twenty years ago." A look of sadness spread over her face.

"You must be an expert in the spell of youth! I would not have taken you for a day over 40!" It was not often Merlin looked amazed, but he did so now. He knew that witches could cast such spells, but they never lasted very long.

"Spell of youth!" said Helen-Joy with a laugh. "I wish. I have no magic powers; I am only a soothsayer. I read the Tarot, look into the crystal ball, and sleep on my pillow of dreams. I merely try to interpret what I see! I have no magic."

"Then who charmed the bindweed to seal your forest, and who released it this morning to allow me entrance?" The old wizard raised an eyebrow quizzically.

Helen-Joy giggled. "Oh, you do look funny when you are in an interrogation mode!"

Merlin felt himself blush. He could not remember the last time that he'd felt his cheeks redden with embarrassment.

"It is not *my* forest. I am just lucky enough to live in this fantastic place! The girls charmed the bindweed to 'seal the forest', as you put it. When I told them you were coming, they charmed the bindweed to open when you arrived and to close again behind you. They can't wait to meet you!

"The girls will be here tonight. They're cooking your dinner. I don't eat meat, but the girls are going to make a barbecue in the garden. They do that every now and again. I supply the wine and the fruit, and we have a good old get-together. Better when Bryan was alive, of course, because he used to play his guitar, and we used to dance and sing. …"

"Excuse me," Merlin interrupted. "Who are 'the girls'?"

"Local coven. There's only seven of them, though. The Bramble family of witches. Really good fun. You're going to enjoy yourself, but you need to get some rest first."

"Helen-Joy, I am sorry but I cannot stay. It is true that I have sought a soothsayer, but I need to search the forest for a dragon's egg which has been stolen. I cannot stay, because I am anxious to get back to work. If we do not find the egg before the next full moon, the dragon may destroy Dalton and every other town in Twydell and Kerner. I beg you to look into your crystal ball and tell me what you see."

"So that's what it's all about," said Helen-Joy. "I could see dragons and flames and floods, but couldn't make sense of it all. I saw you flying round, talking to old King Freddy and then cosying up with the dragons. Where do those giant birds come into the story? I've seen them flying about in my crystal ball a few times, and in my dreams too. It seems they only fly with the rain."

Merlin told Helen-Joy all he knew about the missing egg, beseeching her to help him.

"Best sleep on it!" she declared. "Now take your choice. You can either sleep on the floor in here, or use the hammock in the garden. I'll have a nap and try to put the pieces of all the bits I've seen together. Then we'll party it up with the girls tonight. They'll be able to throw some light on the subject for you, and they can help you search the forest, if you must – but you would be wasting your time. If the egg were here, one of us would know."

Merlin could not argue with his new friend, and he was desperately in need of sleep, so he agreed to Helen-Joy's plan of action.

Helen-Joy led Merlin to the back of her cave.

A bed with satin quilts lay in a cleft at the far end of the cave. Lace curtains separated the bed from the rest of the cave, but Merlin had not realised that the cave turned to the right just in front of the bed. Helen-Joy pulled back heavy red velvet curtains to reveal the beauty of her secret garden.

The garden lay in a hollow inside the mountain, forming its own small valley. Fruit trees grew in abundance, as did vegetables. Flowers of many different varieties and colours flourished. Grapes grew on vines which clung to the side of the tall rocks that surrounded the garden like a wall. A stream ran down the mountainside, into a pool beside which an inviting-looking hammock was strung between two apple trees.

Merlin chose to sleep in the warmth of the afternoon sun. He cast his cloak and hat to one side, and climbed into the hammock. For a while, he listened to the birdsong as he gazed round the secret garden, but his eyelids were heavy, and he soon drifted into the welcome world of slumber.

It was late afternoon when he awoke. It was still warm, and it would have been all too easy to close his eyes again, but he slipped down from the hammock and climbed the stone steps leading back up to the cave.

Helen-Joy had left open the red curtains separating the cave from the garden. He could see her through the lace curtains in front of her bed, lying with a satin sheet across her body. She was fully clothed; she seemed to be in a fitful sleep. Every now and again, she would mutter to herself. It seemed as if she were about to sit up, but then she would simply turn to one side and continue muttering.

Merlin helped himself to a cup of mint tea from the pot which was boiling on the fire. He watched the soothsayer for a while, then made his way back into the garden, ate a ripe peach which he picked from a tree, and then lay back on the hammock and fell asleep again.

The sun was going down, and it was starting to get a bit chilly when Merlin awoke for the second time. He made his way back into the cave. This time, he found Helen-Joy at her table. Tarot cards were spread out in front of her, and the purple cloth had been removed from her crystal ball. She seemed so deep in contemplation that Merlin thought she must be unaware of his presence. However, she told him to help himself to a cup of mint tea, and to pour one for her as well.

She did not thank him as he placed the cup carefully on the table. She simply looked from cards to ball, and back again, just as if she were reading a book. Lifting her cup and sipping the hot brew, she continued to read the tools of her trade.

Finally, she put down her empty cup and smiled at the wizard.

"Yes, I think you are right: the giant birds have stolen the egg. I can see them in some sort of cave. After all, if they bring rain and thunder, they need somewhere to keep dry."

Merlin nodded. What the soothsayer said seemed to make perfect sense.

"They wish the egg no harm. In fact, they seem to love it; but the egg will harm them. Sounds strange, doesn't it? I'm still trying to understand it all." Helen-Joy paused and then added. "There is a lot of sadness. The egg seems to bring them hope, but I am certain that it will harm them!"

"If Ajax or Blitzen find the thunderbirds with their egg, they will certainly harm them!" Merlin stated the obvious.

"No, I don't think Ajax and Blitzen will be the ones to harm the thunderbirds, although I'm sure there would be one almighty scrap if they met!" Helen-Joy pronounced and then said, "The egg is safe, though, and the baby dragon within it is healthy. That's one thing I'm sure about. Anyway, I'll sleep on it again tonight, and, fingers crossed, we might figure out what is going on tomorrow."

Merlin nodded.

"Now. Let's get ready for tonight," Helen-Joy said. "I suggest you have a good old wash, and spruce up. Take those dirty clothes off, and I'll wash them for you. They'll be dry by tomorrow lunchtime, when you set off again. You can wear some of Bryan's old clothes tonight. You're about the same size, so they should fit all right. Even if they don't, it's better than being dirty."

Giving Merlin no chance to reply, she continued. "Have you got a brush or comb for that mop of yours? It looks like you haven't put a brush through it for weeks. I've got some oil you can put in your hair and beard, and that should make it easier for you to comb it through. If you hurry, I'll have time to give you a trim before the party starts."

Merlin was taken aback. No one else had ever spoken to him in the way that Helen-Joy did. Nevertheless, he did as he was told, and felt much better after he had bathed in the stream and combed his hair.

Helen-Joy washed his clothes while he bathed, and seemed to be totally oblivious to the old wizard's nakedness. He wrapped himself in a towel while she cut his hair and beard, and the birds carried away the trimmings to help strengthen their nests. The clothes she found for him fitted him perfectly, and when he looked in her mirror, he considered himself to look ten years younger.

++++++++++++++++++++++++

The girls could be heard before they were seen. Laughter and chatter interrupted the still of the late evening as they wound their way along the forest path. They greeted Merlin with friendly excitement. Their ages ranged from teenager to very old. Merlin found out from talking to the very old cackling witch that they were all related – the Bramble family of witches, just as Helen-Joy had said. The cackling witch was the great-grandmother of the teenage girl. The old witch went on to say that her mother had been banished from Dalton at the same time as Helen-Joy. She and her family had been brought up in the forest, and knew no other life. They felt safe here.

"Tell me, Merlin, are there any more fine-looking wizards like you in Avalon? If there are, send them over here. We've run out of men." The old witch cackled.

"I will tell them of your needs," Merlin said in a joking tone, and the old witch cackled even louder.

"You say that your mother left Dalton with Helen-Joy – so how old is she? She looks so young!"

The cackling never stopped. "She must be, let me see, 106, I think. Ask her yourself!"

"I wouldn't dream of asking a lady how old she is. Are you sure? She's nearly as old as I am, if she's 106!"

"Hey, Helen-Joy, Merlin wants to know how old you are!"

Merlin felt himself blush for the second time that day.

"Hmm .... I lose track a bit, but I'm pretty sure I'm coming up to 107 soon." The soothsayer laughed.

"Good. Another excuse for a party!" called out one of the witches.

"We'll make the cake. You supply the wine!"

"Sounds like a good idea to me!" Helen-Joy laughed. She always seemed to be laughing when she wasn't working.

"Shall we invite Merlin too?" One of the witches spoke loudly, into Helen-Joy's ear, but it was the great-grandmother witch who answered.

"Yes, Merlin will come, and he'll bring along the pick of Avalon's wizards with him!" she said with a cackle.

"Oooh …" replied the girls in unison. "We could do with some men."

Merlin smiled. He wanted to be serious and speak to the witches about the thunderbirds and the lost egg, but he felt that he could not interrupt their party without causing offence. So he settled back on a comfy bench to watch them as they laughed and danced and joked.

However, the great-grandmother sensed his anxiety. She sat herself next to him. "Now don't you worry," she said gently. "While we were preparing dinner, Helen-Joy told me about the egg you seek. I can tell you for sure that it is not in this forest; nor are those birds. If they were here, one of us would've seen 'em.

"We'll come back tomorrow, and all of us together will help piece together this mystery. I don't have too much sympathy for King Freddy or the Daltonians, but I don't suppose I'd like to see young kiddies get hurt.

"I'll get my girls home soon, so they don't suffer with too much of a hangover tomorrow. Even if they do, Helen-Joy's got a good remedy already made up. So don't you worry now, Merlin. You just enjoy yourself tonight and then get a good night's sleep. You need to be well rested because I think you will have a lot of work in front of you. Now then, come and try this rabbit pie I've made. By the way, my name is Bertha."

So Merlin enjoyed his night with the girls. Bertha's home-made rabbit pie was delicious. He ate well and enjoyed a fair amount of home-made wine. By the time the girls left his head was spinning.

Merlin and the soothsayer stood at the entrance to the cave to wave goodbye to the girls. As the darkness of the forest enveloped Bertha and her family, they disappeared from view. However, Merlin could still hear their singing and laughter for several minutes after he lost sight of them. He smiled as he thought of the girls, singing and joking as they made their way home, along the forest paths.

Helen-Joy laid a colourful patchwork quilt on the floor of the cave for Merlin to sleep on, and gave him another quilt with which to cover himself. She then bid him goodnight and went to her bed of dreams.

++++++++++++++++++++++++++++++

The next morning, Merlin awoke to find Helen-Joy again sitting at her table. The Tarot cards were spread in a different arrangement this time. As he stretched, he watched her looking from cards to crystal ball, and back again. He noticed that there was not a grey streak in her brown hair, and he tried to imagine her brown eyes, serious for a change, staring at the images on her cards and into the depths of the glass ball.

She seemed completely oblivious to his presence, but without looking up, she said, "There's hangover remedy in the jug, if you need it, and mint tea in the kettle. Help yourself to anything you want. The unicorns are out front; you might like to go and talk to them, seeing as you know their language. Good idea, that. Go and talk to Lennox. I'm too busy to chat. Give them some of those apples in the bowl by the door. They prefer green ones."

Merlin raised his eyebrows. He hadn't uttered a word, but he did as he was told, smiling as he did so. He tried the hangover remedy, liked its taste, and filled his cup. Picking out a bowl of green apples for the unicorns and a ripe peach for himself, he went outside.

The unicorns lifted their heads from the small patch of grass, and then came towards him expectantly.

"She's a remarkable lady," stated Lennox, as he trotted across the pasture to where Merlin was offering the apples to the mares.

"Remarkable indeed!" Merlin replied.

"The only trouble with this forest is that the bindweed canopy does not allow much sunlight, so there is little grass. The witches have opened it up in small patches so that we get these grazing areas. Helen-Joy feeds us cabbage, carrots, and apples so we don't go hungry."

"Do you never go outside the forest?"

"Rarely, and if we do, it is always at night. The girls are afraid that we might be seen by men, who would then try to enter the forest to catch us. If they did find a way of breaking in, the girls would not be safe either."

"Are there no other people here?"

"No, and no giant birds either. I heard the girls talking about them on the way home last night. There are no giant birds here, my friend, nor a hidden egg. I am sorry you have wasted your time, but perhaps Helen-Joy can help you. Just don't rush her. Now I want you to meet my wives. I have not yet introduced you properly."

Apart from Lennox, the unicorns had never before met anyone who could speak their language. Merlin was enjoying light conversation with the mares when he heard the girls approaching. The laughter and cackling preceded the appearance of the family of seven. The girls waved when they saw the wizard and hurried towards him.

CHAPTER 4

The Bramble Family

"Look how clever he is, talking to the unicorns," one of the witches said.

Merlin heard her clearly; she spoke deliberately loud enough for him to hear.

"Our luck seems to be changing, girls!" said the witch, gesturing towards the unicorns. "First, those lovely creatures find their way here; next, we get a visit from a man!"

Merlin laughed with them, greeting them warmly.

Helen-Joy appeared at the door, with a tray of cups, a jug of the hangover remedy, and pot of mint tea.

Without being asked, Merlin went back into the cave and came back with a bowl of fruit to share.

Helen-Joy smiled.

"Got him trained already," cackled the great-grandmother witch.

They sat on the grass, and Helen-Joy explained what she had seen in her dreams and what the tools of her trade had revealed to her. Most clearly of all, she could see a mountain with a rain cloud hovering over it constantly. She was sure that the egg was safe, but the two giant birds which had stolen it were in danger. She said that Merlin must act swiftly if he was to stop the catastrophe which would occur before the next full moon.

"Unfortunately, girls, Merlin must leave today!" Helen-Joy said.

The girls sighed in unison, and Lennox, who understood the human language but could not speak it, gave a whinny of disappointment.

Merlin asked, "Do any of you know where the mountain with the rain cloud hovering above it lies?"

"None of my family has ever left the forest," replied Great-Grandmother Bramble. "So we wouldn't know."

All the witches, except the youngest, shook their heads.

"I have seen it," said the girl, looking at the ground, as if she were filled with shame.

"How can you, Heather?" exclaimed her mother, who was called Sally. "You have never left the forest!"

"Yes, I have," admitted Heather. "I did not want to be deceitful. I love this forest, but sometimes it feels like a prison. One night, not long ago, when you asked me to open the bindweed for the unicorns and keep guard for them, I borrowed Great-Grandmother's old broomstick. I flew up in the air. I felt like I was free. It was wonderful. I could feel the wind in my face and blowing through my hair."

The older witches gasped, and Sally shook her head in dismay.

"I wasn't gone for long," Heather said in a quiet voice, her head hung low. "I saw a mountain in the moonlight, with a cloud above it. The strange thing is that it was only raining on that one mountain."

"Thank you for being honest," Merlin said gently. "If you had kept your journey a secret, I might not have known that the place I seek is so close."

However, the witches were not so gentle with her.

Sally got up, strode to where her daughter sat, and slapped her hard across the face.

"You foolish girl! Don't you ever do anything so foolish and dangerous again! You know what happened to your father and your uncles! Do you want to disappear too?"

The other witches shouted their agreement, and Heather covered her face and ran inside Helen-Joy's cave.

"She will not do it again without your permission," the soothsayer said. "I saw Heather in my dream that night, although I did not see the mountain of which she speaks. The next day, I told her that she must not go off on her own again."

"She won't go off anywhere again," Heather's grandmother, who was called Nora, said sternly. "Because none of us will ever leave the forest!"

"I can't believe she would do such a thing." Sally shook her head. Her face had turned white. "She knows what happened to her father."

"What did happen to her father?" asked Merlin.

"Well, that's just it – we don't really know!" Great-Grandmother Bramble replied, and then she went on to tell Merlin the history of her family.

The laughing and cackling stopped now, and gloomy expressions replaced smiles. The whole family sat with hunched shoulders as Great-Grandmother Bramble recounted the past.

"My mother and father brought me here as a child. They came with Helen-Joy and her husband, Bryan, when King Freddy's grandfather told all our kind we had to leave Twydell. A wizard and his son already lived here, in the same house where we all live in now. I married Ernie, the son, and we were happy enough. We had two fine daughters: Nora and Maura." She nodded towards each of her daughters. "Maura never married, but Nora found a husband, a good man called Dillbert. He came to the forest from Kerner, seeking refuge, because our kind was being persecuted in Kerner too."

Nora took up the story, with much sorrow in her voice. "Dillbert and I had three beautiful daughters before he died: Dilly, Dally, and Sally."

The three sister witches nodded.

Merlin looked at the three women, all of whom were not just plain, but ugly. *Ah,* he thought. *Beauty is in the eye of the beholder.*

Nora continued. "We thought our daughters would never marry for there were no more men in the forest. But then, one day, a man came to the forest from Dalton. He was the son of a half-witch. He had very little magic in him, but his sons – Jerry, Garod, and Isaiah – had started to do strange things. His wife was horrified, afraid the neighbours would see the boys making their toys fly through the air.

"The father feared for his sons' lives, so he brought them to the forest. Stood outside yelling for a witch, he did. Anyway, he left the boys with us, and Mum and Maura brought them up, just as if they were their own."

The elderly witches nodded, their thoughts lost in the melancholy of remembrance.

"They were good kids. They liked it here in the forest. Their father and mother used to come and visit sometimes. You could see they really loved their sons. If they didn't love them, they wouldn't have brought them here, would they?"

The question didn't require an answer, but everyone, including Merlin, nodded in agreement.

"The boys were happy enough, and they married my girls," said Nora. "But their parents stopped visiting. We didn't know why. One day, the boys decided that they hadn't seen their parents for a long while, and thought they'd walk into Dalton to find them. Heather was already born, and Isaiah wanted to tell his parents that he had a child. The boys promised they would do no magic when they got to Dalton because they didn't want to draw any attention to themselves. The last thing they wanted was to cause trouble. So, off they went, but they never returned. We think the people of Dalton must have recognised them and killed them."

"Or they might have found some other women and stayed with them!" snapped Dilly.

"Speak for yourself," retorted Sally angrily. "My husband would never have left me! He loved me, and he loved our daughter!"

"Stop this!" Helen-Joy broke into the argument. "I can tell you this. Your husbands did not abandon you willingly. They all loved you, and they wanted to return to the forest. The forest was their home! I know this, but I cannot tell you any more."

"Can't, or won't?" asked Nora Bramble. "You have said this before, but you never tell us what happened to them. I can only believe that your reluctance to tell us means that they are dead."

Helen-Joy hung her head low but did not reply.

Merlin saw the great sadness that the girls suffered. They had laughed and joked the night before, but now they were filled with anguish.

"I do not know what happened to your husbands," he said. "But if I am successful in my mission, I will not be afraid to ask King Frederrick for the truth. If I finish this mission alive, I promise that I will come back and tell you what, if anything, I have found out."

"Thank you, Merlin." Great-Grandmother Bramble looked into the wizard's face. "You are a good man. I would like to know what happened to our boys before I die. I can't say it will make me die in peace, but not knowing is what makes it so difficult."

Maura wrapped her arms round her mother, holding the old witch close.

Merlin felt helpless. He tried to think of something to do or say to lift the unhappiness which now weighed so heavily in the air.

Helen-Joy tried to lighten the mood. "Girls, Merlin has to be on his way. Sally, will you let Heather go with him to the edge of the forest to point him in the direction of the mountain with the rain cloud hovering above it?"

"To the edge." Sally wiped the tears from her eyes and looked up. "But not an inch farther!"

"Thank you, Sally." Merlin smiled at her. "I would appreciate your daughter's help."

"So, now it is time to pack your things and go, Merlin," Helen stated firmly. She reached into the pocket of her smock and pulled out a sealed piece of parchment. "I know that you want to ask me if your mission will be successful. If I tell you I think it will be successful, you may be overconfident. If I tell you it won't, then you might give up. What I think may not even be right. So, I have written what I predict in this parchment, but you must swear, in front of the girls, not to open it until your work is complete."

"Very wise," murmured Great-Grandmother Bramble.

The other witches murmured their agreement.

Merlin raised his right hand and smiled. "I swear most solemnly, in front of the Bramble family of witches who reside in the Forbidden Forest, not to open the parchment till my mission is over, one way or another."

"Well, let's get you packed and ready to go!" said Helen-Joy as she hurried back to the cave, disappearing behind the waterfall.

Lennox trotted up beside Merlin. The unicorn's chestnut mare with the white blaze stood a little way behind.

"We are not beasts of burden, but you may ride on my back one more time, my wise wizard," Lennox said. "Sheba, one of my mares, will take the young witch."

"That is most kind," Merlin said in Unicornian, bowing his head in thanks to the beautiful mare.

The mare lowered her head in acknowledgement.

Merlin told the witches that Sheba would allow Heather to ride on her back.

The witches clapped their hands with glee.

Although Sally's eyes still glistened with tears, she gave a wide smile at the honour bestowed on her daughter.

"What a privilege!" sighed Nora, the proud grandmother of Heather.

Merlin packed his things.

Helen-Joy rolled up some leafless bindweed into a ball, like string. She insisted that Merlin take it, although she could give no reason why.

Without bothering to ask questions, the sorcerer dutifully placed the ball of bindweed in his pocket. *A ball of string in one's pocket is always handy. I can always find a use for it,* he reasoned to himself.

The wizard said his goodbyes, genuinely sorry to leave. Helen-Joy waved goodbye from the waterfall, but the Bramble family ran behind the trotting unicorns for as far as they could keep pace. The misery of earlier had left them. They were now in high spirits as they watched Heather bobbing up and down on Sheba's back, holding tightly to her mane. The young witch's face beamed with delight as she clung to the unicorn.

At the edge of the forest, Heather pointed towards the mountain beneath the hovering rain cloud.

Merlin could just see the strange spectacle, between the passing white clouds.

He boarded Willy's broomstick, but before he set off, he made Heather promise that she would go straight home. Steering his conveyance towards the mountain, he turned only to wave goodbye to the young witch and the two unicorns.

CHAPTER 5

Storm and Thor's Folly

It took Merlin little more than an hour to reach the mountain upon which the rain poured. Pulling up his collar and wrapping his travelling cloak round himself in an effort to keep dry, he circled round, trying to locate the entrance to a cave. As he wound his broom round the top of the mountain, he smelt the unpleasant stench of burning. Wiping the rain from his eyes and squinting, he thought he could see smoke coming out of a narrow crevice. He dipped the broom and landed on a slippery ledge just outside the opening.

The smell was far worse as he reached the entrance to the cave, making the old wizard gag; nevertheless, he rushed inside. Two giant birds were flapping their burning wings and tail feathers in terror. They were trying to get outside and into the rain, but a small, fiery dragon, breathing flames, stood in front of them.

The small green dragon was having great fun. It was setting fire to a large nest which stood in the middle of the cave, burning it a bit at a time, blowing out the flames, and then reigniting them. The creature seemed completely unaware of the deadly state of affairs in which it had placed the birds.

With one hand, Merlin used his cloak to cover his mouth. With the other, he raised his staff to quench the flames devouring the nest. Next, he issued a stunning spell on the tiny dragon, which rendered it motionless. Finally, he put out the flames burning the birds' wings.

"Quickly!" he spluttered. The smoke was getting into Merlin's lungs, his eyes were stinging, and he was starting to choke. "Get outside, and let the rain cool your wings!" He managed to shout between coughs, hoping the language he used was one the birds would understand. He was not sure whether they understood him or simply acted on instinct to half fly, half race out into the rain.

He looked at the ashes of the nest and saw the remains of a broken egg. *Well, little fellow – or perhaps it's little lady – you have arrived early. You are still supposed to be in your shell for a few more weeks yet.* He checked the tiny motionless creature, to make sure that it was all right, before picking it up and rushing outside.

In the open air, the thunderbirds were languishing in the rain. Merlin coughed and spluttered, but, after taking a few deep breaths of fresh air, he eventually managed to speak.

"What, in heaven's name, made you steal the dragon's egg?" Merlin asked angrily from the shelter of the cave entrance. He held his staff ready to cast another spell if either of the birds attacked him. However, the large creatures looked petrified as they stood on the ledge, allowing the cool rain to soothe their wings.

"We had no egg of our own," replied the male. "There are so few of us left, and we wanted children so badly. One day, we were sheltering in a cave near the lake. We saw the dragons approaching the same cave. We did not know whether they would attack us, so we hid at the back. We heard them talking about the egg they were expecting, and we thought how lucky they were. We followed them back to their cave. We kept a good distance behind them, and they were so absorbed in each other's company that they did not see us. When we got home, we talked about taking the egg to make it our own. The dragons would have another sooner or later, and then they wouldn't miss the one we took."

"Fools!" bellowed Merlin. "Dragons only usually have one egg in a lifetime! You have caused the deaths of many people, and rendered others homeless. On top of that, when the dragons find out what you have done, they will no longer unleash their vengeance on the people of Twydell and Kerner. They will unleash their vengeance on you!"

The birds squawked in alarm.

"We are sorry," replied the female. "I wanted an egg so badly. I had heard of a bird called the cuckoo, which always lays its eggs in another bird's nest. I always wanted to come home and find that a cuckoo had visited my nest and left its egg behind.

"I have been obsessed with the thought of having an egg of my own. I was envious of the dragons, and I found a little place in the mountains from where I could keep watch on their cave.

"One day, I saw the green dragon fly off, and sometime afterwards I saw the blue one go down to the lake. I knew where the entrance to the cave was, so I decided to pop in to take a look at their nest. I only intended looking, but when I saw the egg, I fell in love with it. It was such a big egg, just like the one I always wished I would be blessed with. I couldn't resist it. I picked it up in my talons and carried it home."

"What could I do?" asked the male. "Of course, I was worried when I saw that she had actually taken the egg. We had talked about stealing it, but I never thought that we would really do such a thing. The idea of stealing someone else's egg was more of a game. Once it was taken, I couldn't risk taking it back, chancing the dragons' anger, could I? It is true we both wanted an egg, and I agreed to keep it. We didn't know that dragons could only have one egg, though.

"We took good care of it, but when it hatched … well, you can see for yourself. We did not expect the fire.

"We never thought that the little thing would breathe fire before we could train it. I am sorry about the people who suffered the dragons' anger, but if people had their way, we would already be dead. Our kind is not wanted here!"

Merlin sighed. "Our kind is not wanted here. How often have I heard that?"

After a moment, he added, "I must return the baby to its parents before the stunning spell wears off; otherwise, the creature will set me alight too. I noticed you have plenty of food stored."

"Yes," replied the male. "We stocked up well to prepare for our … I mean 'the' baby."

"Well, I suggest you stay in the cave, and do not attempt to go outside till your wings and tail feathers are regrown.

The dragons know that it was you who stole their child, and they are looking for you."

The birds looked shocked. For a long while, they stood stock-still, frozen with fear at the thought of being the target of a dragon's fury.

Merlin continued, still very cross himself. "I will tell the dragons that you kept the egg safe, believing it was one you lost. I will tell them that you gave the baby to me willingly when you realised the egg it hatched from was not yours. I will tell them that you flew off towards the ocean, saying that you would not return here again. I suggest that, when your feathers grow back, you do just that – fly far away, where the dragons cannot find you."

"Thank you, strange man," said the male as he closed his singed wings gently round his wife, who nodded her head in quiet acquiescence to Merlin's plan.

"Now I must leave, or this little perisher will roast me alive on our way back to its parents. I don't want to issue another stunning spell on it again, in case I harm it."

The wizard suddenly realised why Helen-Joy had given him the twine. Taking it out of his pocket, he wound it round the tiny dragon's snout and tied it securely. He then picked up the little creature, got on the broomstick, and left the thunderbirds still standing in the rain on the wet ledge.

The wizard travelled as fast as he could. As he sped through the air, he felt the baby dragon start to move. He held it tight and was relieved to find that it fell into a natural slumber. *It must be the motion of the broom, rocking slightly in the evening breeze, that is lulling the baby to sleep,* he thought.

It was the middle of the night when Merlin dipped the broom towards the dragon's cave. A warm glow exuded from the entrance. As he landed, the baby awoke and made a simpering noise. He loosened the twine from round its snout, and as he entered the cave, he set the child free.

There was a fire in the middle of the room within the cave. Ajax was lying at the other side of the room, his wings wrapped round Blitzen, who rested her head against his muscular shoulder.

They both looked up when they heard Merlin approaching, and they gasped with joy when they saw their child trotting along in front of the wizard.

The child headed straight towards the fire, which seemed to attract it like a magnet. In no time at all, the small creature was soon breathing out its own fiery breath, so that flame met flame.

The dragons arose, as if in one movement, and rushed, one either side of the fire, to greet their offspring. They blew warm air from their nostrils over the tiny green creature, and licked it with such powerful strokes that the child kept falling from one of its parent's tongues to the other.

Merlin smiled. "I shall leave you. The thunderbirds who took your egg are sorry." He told the dragons the tale he had concocted with the thunderbirds. He did not think that the dragons altogether believed him, but they were too busy fondling their child to argue.

"Thank you, Merlin." Blitzen's voice was barely a murmur. A large teardrop slid down her leathery blue face and onto the baby's head, extinguishing a small flame emitting from its nostril.

"If I can do anything for you at any time, Merlin," said Ajax, "you know that I am indebted to you. We have kept our side of the agreement and have not unleashed any more of our wrath on the Twydellers or Kernans."

"I am glad to hear it," said Merlin. Not wishing to intrude any further on this, their special time, he turned to leave the dragon family.

The dragons, including the baby, who trotted along in front of its parents, followed Merlin to wave their goodbyes.

In its excitement, the baby dragon let forth a flame which caught the brush end of Merlin's – or, rather, Willy's – broom.

Merlin stamped on the broom, swiftly putting out the flames.

"Oh, dear, I hope it will be all right!" exclaimed Ajax.

"Oh, I'm sure it will be," replied Merlin politely, very much doubting his own words.

He launched the broom from the ledge outside the cave, immediately feeling it plummet. He managed to bring it back up, and waved to the family of dragons silhouetted against the firelight of the cave. The broom then plummeted again.

As the broom rose and fell sharply, over and over again, the dragons thought Merlin was just showing off his flying expertise.

"Look at that!" said Ajax. "He really knows how to fly that thing."

Ajax and Blitzen turned, taking their child back into the warmth of its rightful home.

CHAPTER 6

The Soothsayer's Predictions

Merlin had a difficult ride back to the capital of Twydell. Throughout the flight, the broom shuddered and lost altitude, regaining its height only to lose it again. However, it managed the journey back to Dalton safely.

The guards had spotted the broom and its passenger in the distance, as dawn was breaking, and summoned the king. By the time Merlin landed somewhat ungracefully in the courtyard, the king was waiting for him.

In between gulps of breakfast, Merlin told King Frederrick about the events of the last few days. Merlin hadn't realised how hungry he was. He finished with gusto the plate of bacon, sausages, and egg, and was just wiping the plate clean with a piece of bread when he remembered the parchment.

While the king was dictating a message to his secretary, to send the good news to all the towns and villages in Twydell,

Merlin opened the sealed parchment to read Helen-Joy's prediction:

1. Your mission will be successful, and you will return the baby dragon to its parents. You will earn their gratitude, and one day you will ask them to repay the debt.

2. The three men who left the Forbidden Forest – Jerry, Garod, and Isaiah – are suffering much harm in a prison dungeon. They are so weak that they have lost their magic powers. Please ask the king to release them and let them come home.

3. You will come back to the Forbidden Forest, but first you must waste no time in returning to Avalon.

Merlin was stunned. He felt sickened to think that three wizards might be imprisoned in the dungeon below the very palace in which he was enjoying hospitality. He sat staring at the parchment.

The king turned away from his secretary and started talking to Merlin again. Frederrick expressed his gratitude to Merlin, promising him anything he wanted.

Just then, Merlin raised his head. The stern manner in which Merlin looked directly into the king's face startled the king because, up to this point, their talk had been amicable.

Merlin's voice was loud, and his tone was no longer friendly. "I believe you hold three of my kind – three wizards – in your dungeon cells. I ask you to release them and give them safe passage back to the Forbidden Forest."

"You are wrong, Merlin," stated the king. He looked bewildered but spoke his words firmly. "It is true I have had no love for your kind in the past. My people have never liked those of magic. However, we do not harm anyone unless they do wrong. My ancestors ordered all those with magic powers out of Dalton and all our other towns and villages. But, to my knowledge – and I am willing to take oath and swear – no person of magic has ever been harmed."

Merlin looked into the king's eyes. He felt puzzled because Helen-Joy had been right about everything else, and yet he felt sure that the king was telling the truth.

"The wizards, whose names are Jerry, Garod, and Isaiah, were travelling to Dalton to visit those they knew. They never returned to their wives, who live in the forest. It is those same women, all of whom are witches, who have helped me to find the dragon child."

"I swear I know nothing of these missing magic men," King Frederrick reiterated. "But I make this oath, on my children's lives, that I will try to find out what has happened to them. It would be a small thing to repay such a large debt, but I cannot promise I will find them. Furthermore, I will issue an order stating that people of magic must no longer be shunned from our towns and villages. They must be treated with respect."

"I believe you," said Merlin, and the coldness left his eyes. He did not wish to linger any longer, because Helen-Joy's message had urged him to return to Avalon. He asked the king to lend him a horse, as his broom had been badly burnt by the baby dragon.

"The least I can do, my good fellow." Frederrick beamed, delighted that he could reward the wizard in some way for his services.

Whilst the king's staff busied about, organising a horse and escort for the wizard, the king took the opportunity to tell Merlin about the royal family.

Merlin responded by telling the king more about Arthur and Avalon.

At last, the hurried preparations for Merlin's departure were ready. Merlin was presented with a fine white stallion, which he called Comet. An escort of six soldiers had been arranged to ensure the wizard's safe journey through Twydell and back to Avalon.

As Merlin was about to leave, King Frederrick called him back. "I have been thinking about these missing magic men. Although I am unaware of any Twydeller harming a person of magic, I am aware that King Jeffrey of Kerner offered a reward for any such persons."

"Alive or dead," Frederrick added after a pause, and Merlin saw the shame in the king's eyes.

"Bounty hunters crossed the borders into Twydell. For their reward, they took some people of magic who had been living in the mountains back to Kerner. I am sorry to say I did nothing to stop them."

Merlin sighed, but he appreciated the king's honesty.

The king continued. "I will send a messenger to King Jeffrey forthwith, asking him if the men you seek are there and further asking him to release them into my custody. I shall make it clear that Kerner is as much in your debt as Twydell. If he releases the prisoners, I will tell my men to deliver them safely back to the Forbidden Forest."

“Thank you, sire,” said Merlin. “I do not like what I have heard, but I respect your honesty. I hope you will also bid Jeffrey to release any persons of magic or soothsayers he might hold in his cells.”

“I will indeed; that I promise,” said the king, looking Merlin straight in the eye.

At that, with goodbyes said, Merlin mounted Comet, escorted by six of the king’s men, and made his way back to Merlport. The strangely clad man with straggly hair, whom the kings’ guards had shunned on his first visit to the palace, was now leaving as an honoured foreign diplomat.

CHAPTER 7

Merlin Ends His Tale

Merlin finished telling his tale to the Avalonians.

Esmerelda, the new Queen of the Witches, looked severe. "These men must be found and released. I sincerely hope that this Jeffrey has no more of our kind held in his torture dungeons. I should like to meet this evil man."

"I agree," Merlin said with a sigh. "He may not be evil, but he is certainly blind and unknowing. *If* King Jeffrey holds the brothers, as we suspect he does, then let us hope King Frederrick can persuade him to set them free. Of course, we do not know for sure that they are in a Kerner prison – or, indeed, any prison. We only have Helen-Joy's prediction."

"Your soothsayer seems to have been extremely accurate in her predictions so far." King Allarond's tiny elf voice joined the conversation.

"Yes, well, she's certainly right that I will return to the Forbidden Forest," said Merlin. "I owe Helen-Joy my gratitude. She probably already knows what has happened since I left. Nevertheless, I will return and tell the soothsayer and the Bramble family all that I know. They deserve to be kept informed."

"As soon as our brothers and sisters here have recovered from the battle with the Trajaens, we will send visitors to our sisters in the Forbidden Forest." Esmerelda remained very serious.

"Oh, I agree! It is most important that we do so! The people who live in the Forbidden Forest are happy in their own company, but I know they would appreciate the opportunity to make new friends." Merlin remembered watching the lonely figure of the young witch, Heather, waving to him as he left the forest.

"Yes, you must return to Twydell," stated King Arthur. "I am interested to hear what Frederrick thinks of my offer of Rosalie's hand to his son Derrick. That is, *if* they like each other. Such an alliance will truly strengthen both our countries."

The group stared at Arthur, unaware of the potential marriage contract which Merlin had suggested to Arthur the previous night.

In particular, Prince Edward looked bewildered. He could not believe that his young half-sister might soon be betrothed.

King Arthur, aware of his audience's surprise, continued speaking to hold that attention. "Merlin has already shown the Twydellers the power of magic. The Twydell soldiers will tell their countrymen how well the people of magic, and those without magic, fought alongside each other yesterday. Let us hope that our neighbours will learn how strong our combined forces can be. I still believe we can create a land where we can all live in peace beside each other."

The other leaders nodded their agreement, for this was their ultimate aim.

+++++++++++++++++

Edward waited for the others to leave before asking his father, "Is there anything you wish to tell me?"

Arthur smiled at his son. He told Edward about King Frederrick's offer of the hand of his daughter, Princess Jeanette. Edward breathed a sigh of relief to learn that his father had turned down the offer and not tried to force him into a marriage he did not want. The fact that his father had recognised his love for Daisy took a huge weight off Edward's shoulders. He had feared that his father would oppose a relationship with the so-called wild girl from the mountains. The other burdens he carried since the losses in the battle with the Trajaens were heavy enough.

Edward was in love. He thought he had hidden the feelings he felt so deeply in his heart. But, if his father had seen through him, other people would as well. He knew he must tell Daisy how he felt.

However, despite his relief that his father had accepted his love for Daisy, Edward had a new concern. He was worried that his little half-sister might soon be encouraged to wed someone she did not like. If Rosalie did not like Derrick, and did not wish to marry him, Edward would defend her decision.

More from the *Tales of Avalon* Series:

The New Land, is the first book in the *Tales of Avalon* Series. It was published in 2016.

What happened to Arthur, King of the Britons, after he was allegedly killed on the battlefield? Legend has it that Merlin, the mighty sorcerer, put the king's body in a boat and set it sail for a mysterious place called Avalon. However, many Britons refused to accept that Arthur was really dead: instead believing that Merlin had taken the king to a place of safety. There have been many theories as to the whereabouts of Avalon, but none proved to be accurate.

The New Land is the first book in the *Tales of Avalon* series. It tells the story of how Arthur, magical beings, and other Britons, who feared for their lives, sought refuge in a far-off land. They hoped their new home would be a place where magical beings and humans could live together in peace and harmony. Did the travellers find the new life they so desired? Well, they certainly found a land full of surprise and adventure.

The Avalonians soon find that they have to form new and unusual alliances in order to protect themselves against an unexpected enemy.

If you like stories about witches, wizards, fairies, elves, giants, and unicorns, you will enjoy this book.

The Exchange of Rings, is the third book in the *Tales of Avalon* Series. It was published in 2016.

The Exchange of Rings follows on from *The New Land* the first book in the series. It describes the preparations for the wedding of Princess Jeanette of Twydell to Prince Steven of Kerner. Rosalie is excited at the prospect of meeting Derrick, Prince of Twydell, who many hope will be her future husband. The weddings are an opportunity for each county to build new alliances.

Everything seems to be running smoothly but news is brought that wizards, who have been missing from Twydell's Forbidden Forest for many years, are being held in a Kerner prison. It is also revealed that fairies and elves have also been treated with cruelty by Kernans. The magical people of Avalon are furious and some want to take revenge on Kerner.

King Arthur of Avalon, Merlin the wizard, and their new found ally King Frederrick of Twydell, try to resolve situation. They are concerned that revenge will be the beginning of war.

The allies hope that a solution can be found when the King of Kerner is forced to ask the magical people, of the Forbidden Forest, for help.

A Story Never to be Told, is the fourth book in the *Tales of Avalon* Series. It is to be published in early 2017.

What happened to Azgoose, the clever old witch, who created the clouds of goo which delayed the Trajaens at the Battle of Merlport? Although the Avalonians sent out search parties, she was not found.

In *A Story Never to be Told* secrets continue to unfold. In this book we meet the Rabbart lll, the powerful King of Barrmin, and his family. King Rabbart rules all the former kingdoms and tribes in the northern lands.

King Rabbart befriends Arthur and the magical people of Avalon. He offers one of his beautiful daughters in marriage to Edward.

Is Rabbart lll's friendship with Avalon sincere? Will Edward remain loyal to Daisy, or will he marry a Princess of Barrmin to strengthen the alliance between the two countries?

The answers can only be found in *A Story Never to Be Told.*

ABOUT THE AUTHOR

Daisy Bourne was born in 1917. She was unofficially adopted by a farmer and his wife, and her name was changed when she was very young. I am very proud to use my mother's birth name as a pseudonym when writing the *Tales of Avalon* series.

Later in life, my mum again took up the rural lifestyle she had known as a child. As a child, I, too, enjoyed spending time in the fields with our cows, pigs, goats, and chicken. That's me in the photo, around 1955, sitting on a cow's back.

One of Mum's talents was to read tea leaves and playing cards. People often used to knock at the door and ask for a reading. We used to be fascinated by the way she articulated what she saw in the cards and the teacups.

Mum's seventh child was a girl whom she named Helen Joyce (we know her as Joy). Joy inherited some of Mum's talents and is an internationally known clairvoyant and Tarot reader. In this second book in the *Tales of Avalon* series, I introduce Helen-Joy, the soothsayer – and, yes, some of the character is based on my little sister.

Lightning Source UK Ltd.
Milton Keynes UK
UKOW02f0844121016

285064UK00001B/30/P